"I hate you, Mom!"

A story of unconditional love

Story
Yumi Hopfner

Illustration
Jaime Hoffman

I hate you, Mom!
Copyright © 2018 by Yumi Hopfner

All rights reserved. No part of this publication may be reproduced, distributed, or transmitted in any form or by any means, including photocopying, recording, or other electronic or mechanical methods, without the prior written permission of the author, except in the case of brief quotations embodied in critical reviews and certain other non-commercial uses permitted by copyright law.

Tellwell Talent
www.tellwell.ca

978-0-2288-0368-3 (Paperback)

To my Mom, Dad,
loving husband,
and beautiful children
who inspire me to live,
love, and learn
one present moment
at a time.

One beautiful summer night,
Felicity was having so much fun
playing in her back yard,
until Mom came and said:

"Felicity, it's time to come inside.
It's time to go to bed."

"Can I play bit longer? I'm having **so much fun**, and I really, **really** want to play!"

"I know you are having **so much fun**, but sweetie, it's time to go to bed."

Before she even knew it, Felicity's heart filled with disappointment and anger, and she yelled, "**I hate you, mom**!

You are the worst mom ever!"

Mom **paused** and took
a long deep breath.

"I'm sorry you feel that way.
I love you."

Mom **paused** and took
another long deep breath.

"Call me when you are calm
and ready for your bedtime,"
said Mom gently,
and she went back inside.

Felicity stood there, alone.

The sound of her voice yelling "I hate you, mom!" echoed in her head.

She stood there for a little longer, until the echo faded away.

She took **a long deep breath**.

As her head started to clear, she noticed that the sky was getting dark.

She realized that she was actually feeling a bit tired.

She remembered how much she loved reading with Mom at bedtime.

She took **another long deep breath**.

Even though she still felt angry, she decided to go inside.

Alone in her room,
Felicity put on her pyjamas
and chose some books for bedtime,
just like she always did.

But tonight was **different**.

She was still **angry** that
she had to stop playing
when she was having **so much fun**,
and she also felt **so yucky**
about yelling "**I hate you, mom**!"

Felicity took **a long deep breath**.

"Mom, I chose my books. I'm ready," she said quietly.

When Mom came and sat down right next to Felicity on the bed, Felicity was quiet for a moment.

Then, she took another long deep breath.

"Mom...?"

"What, Felicity?"

"I'm **sorry** I said I hate you… I was just so angry."

"I know. You were having **so much fun** and you **really** wanted to keep playing.

You were angry and disappointed because you had to stop playing and come inside. Thank you for your apology.

I love you always."

"Do you love me
when I'm angry with you?"

Felicity asked Mom.

"Yes, I love you even when you are angry with me.

My love for you is stronger than anger."

"How about when I don't listen? Do you love me when I don't listen?"

Felicity asked Mom.

"Yes, I love you even when you don't listen.

My love for you is stronger than any bad choices you make," said Mom with a smile.

"How about when I tell you I hate you?" Felicity whispered.

"Yes, I love you always.

My love for you is stronger than hurtful words you choose to say," Mom whispered softly.

"When I'm sad?"

"Yes, I love you when you're sad."

Mom touched Felicity's cheek ever so gently, as if she was wiping away her tears.

"When I whine?"

"Yes, I love you even when you whine," said Mom in an extra whiny voice that made Felicity laugh.

"When I'm grumpy?"

"Yes, I love you even when you're grumpy," said Mom, making a grumpy old face that made Felicity giggle.

"My love for you is stronger than anything in the whole wide world.

My love is **always there, no matter what**," said Mom.

Felicity and mom looked at each other for a moment until warm smiles spread over their faces.

Felicity didn't feel angry anymore.

**She felt love.
She felt loved.**

"Mom, guess what?
We forgot **all** about my books!"

"That's true!" said Mom.

They chuckled together softly.

"What do you say?
Shall we read them now, sweetie?"
asked Mom.

"Hmmmm… no…
you know why, Mom?"

"Why?" asked Mom, surprised.

"**Because tonight you told me
the story of love!**"
said Felicity with a big smile.

"I sure did, didn't I?"

"That's my new favourite bedtime story," Felicity and Mom said at the exact same time.

They looked at each other
and giggled warmly.

"Goodnight, Mom;

I love you."

About the Author

Yumi, a Registered Doctoral Psychologist with a Ph.D. in Clinical Psychology, is licensed to practice in Saskatchewan and Alberta, Canada. She is currently practicing at her private practice in Saskatchewan, providing psychological counselling services to children, adults, and families. She is also a mother of two young children. Creating children's books that inspire children, parents, families, and professionals has always been one of her passions.

About the Story

One of the many challenges we face as parents at some points in our parenting journey is the moment when our children choose "revenge" as their goal of misbehaviour.* In short, a child acts from the principle of "I'm hurting, so I hurt you." In these challenging moments filled with raw emotions, we as parents often get sucked into the intensity and we take it personally, feeling attacked and hurt. As a result, we tend to react with the same revenge principle, failing to respond calmly with love. Your children, you, and the parent-child relationship are all hurt in the process.

It is my hope that this story inspires children, parents, and families to appreciate those intense moments as great opportunities to learn about unconditional love. Use these challenges as stepping stones to continue nurturing relationships of trust.

When children have opportunities to experience "unconditional love" with you in action, they not only learn to love you and others unconditionally, but they also learn to love themselves unconditionally.

The gift of unconditional self-love can offer a healthier and more balanced foundation for our children as they continue to explore their life journey ahead.

* *"Revenge" is listed as one of the four goals of misbehaviour in Adlerian Child Guidance Principles, according to Don Dinkmeyer, Sr., Gary D. McKay, and Don Dinkmeyer, Jr. (1979). Systematic Training for Effective Parenting (STEP). New York, NY: Random House.*

CPSIA information can be obtained
at www.ICGtesting.com
Printed in the USA
LVHW07n2005260918
591505LV00003B/3/P